TOPSY A

STAY WITH A FRIEND

Jean and Gareth Adamson

Blackie

Copyright © 1987 Jean and Gareth Adamson

British Library Cataloguing in Publication Data
Adamson, Jean
Topsy and Tim stay with a friend.
I.   Title   II. Adamson, Gareth
823'.914[J]   PZ7

ISBN 0-216-92315-8
ISBN 0-216-92316-6 Pbk

Blackie and Son Limited
7 Leicester Place
London WC2H 7BP

Printed in Great Britain by
Thomson Litho Ltd, East Kilbride, Scotland

Dring-dring! Dring-dring! went
the telephone in Topsy and Tim's
house.
'Topsy! Tim!' shouted Mummy. 'It's
Tony's mum on the phone. Would
you like to go to tea with Tony
and stay the night?'
'YES, PLEASE!' shouted the twins.

They ran upstairs to start packing. Soon there were two enormous piles of clothes and toys on the floor.

'You won't need all that,' said Mummy. 'You are only going for one night.'

Topsy and Tim started all over again. They each packed their washing things and toothbrushes, their pyjamas and a change of clean clothes.

'Do you want to take your dear
old teddies?' asked Mummy. 'You
like to cuddle them at bedtime.'
'No,' said Tim. 'Tony will laugh
at us if we take teddies to bed with us.'

Dad took them along to Tony's house. Tony and his mum were waiting for them. Tony was very excited.

'Come upstairs and see where you are going to sleep,' he said to Topsy and Tim.
They all raced upstairs.
'Be good,' Dad called up after them.

There was a put-you-up bed
in Tony's room, beside Tony's
bed.
'That's for Tim to sleep in,'
said Tony.
'Where's my bed?' asked Topsy.

Topsy's bed was in the spare room.
It was quite a small room, but it
looked very cosy.
They tested Topsy's bed for
bouncability.
Tony's mum came upstairs.
'Tea is ready children,' she said.

Tony's mum gave them all the
things they liked best for tea.
'It's like a party,' said Topsy.
'It *is* a party,' said Tony.

After tea Topsy and Tim and Tony
went out to play in the garden.
It was a wild and weedy garden.
'Let's play LOST IN THE JUNGLE,'
said Tony.

Tony showed them an old pond
behind a bush. There wasn't
much water in it, just a lot of
mud. They stirred the mud with
sticks.

'I can see a crocodile!' said
Topsy. But it wasn't a crocodile.
It was a hoppity frog—and it
gave Topsy such a surprise that
she sat down PLONK in the mud.

Topsy had never been so muddy before. She had muddy hands and muddy feet and her clothes were all muddy, too. She began to howl.

Tony's mum came running to see
what was wrong.
'I want my Mummy!' sobbed Topsy.
'I think you want a bath!' laughed
Tony's mum.

Tony's mum was as kind as kind could be. She put Topsy into a warm, bubbly bath and soon she was nice and clean again. As it was nearly bedtime Topsy got into her pyjamas. She was glad she had brought some clean clothes for the next day.

Tony's mum called the boys in.
They were rather muddy, too.
'We've had a lovely time,' said
Tim.
'I can see you have,' said Tony's
mum.
Tony and Tim took turns in the
shower.

When Tony's mum came to tuck
them into bed, Tony was lying
down cuddling a big, old teddy
bear. Tim was sitting up in his
bed and he didn't look very happy.
'Are you all right, Tim?' asked
Tony's mum.

'I want to go
home,' said Tim.
'Oh dear!' said
Tony's mum kindly.
'Tim is feeling
home-sick.'

Topsy came to help cheer Tim
up—and she was carrying her
dear old teddy.
'I wish I'd brought *my* teddy,'
said Tim.
'You have,' said Topsy. 'He's
in your bag. Mummy packed our
teddies after all.'

Soon Topsy and Tim and Tony
were all tucked up with their
dear old teddies beside them.
'Sleep well, children,' said
Tony's mum. 'We'll have lots
of fun tomorrow.'

Tony's mum closed their
bedroom doors and went
downstairs. A few minutes
later Tony's door opened
and in came Topsy.
'I don't feel like going
to sleep,' she said.

Tony and Tim didn't feel sleepy
either. Soon they were having
a wonderful game of rabbit
burrows in the beds.

When Tony's mum looked in later
that night, Tony's bedroom was
in an awful mess—but Topsy
and Tim and Tony were all fast
asleep. And their teddies were
too.